Thomas P. Slider

Memoirs of General William Butler

Including a brief sketch of his father and brother, who fell in the

revolution, at Cloud's Creek, Lexington District, S. C

Thomas P. Slider

Memoirs of General William Butler
Including a brief sketch of his father and brother, who fell in the revolution, at Cloud's Creek, Lexington District, S. C

ISBN/EAN: 9783337224752

Printed in Europe, USA, Canada, Australia, Japan

Cover: Foto ©Raphael Reischuk / pixelio.de

More available books at **www.hansebooks.com**

OF

GENERAL WILLIAM BUTLER.

Including a Brief Sketch of his Father and Brother,
who fell in the Revolution, at Cloud's
Creek, Lexington District, S. C.

Together with Incidents, Anecdotes and Stirring Events
Connected with his Life.

ATLANTA, GEORGIA:
Jas. P. Harrison & Co., Printers and Binders.
1885.

MEMOIRS

OF

GENERAL WILLIAM BUTLER.

Including a Brief Sketch of his Father and Brother,
who fell in the Revolution, at Cloud's
Creek, Lexington District, S. C.

Together with Incidents, Anecdotes and Stirring Events
Connected with his Life.

ATLANTA, GEORGIA :
JAS. P. HARRISON & CO., PRINTERS AND BINDERS.
1885.

To the young men of our common country, who are coming forward to the front and pressing onward, that they may read and behold the sterling qualities of true and noble manhood; the stern, patriotic virtues of men who stood steadfast and firm throughout the momentous struggle that tried men's souls; remembering that if disaster comes to the country, it must come over the ruins of the noble characters in our history. It must come trampling on the memories of Washington, Jefferson, Marion, Sumter, Butler and others. Before the patriotic instincts can be weakened and overcome, your reverence for those and other great men must be destroyed. You must be made ashamed of their achievements, and their grand sentiments must find no echo in your hearts. Here you will find food for study, food for admiration and food for example and ambition, ever teaching the watchword of the true American citizen,

" Dare to do right and trust the consequences to God."

TO SOUTH CAROLINA.

" Sweet clime of my kindred, blest land of my birth
The fairest, the dearest, the brightest on earth !
Where'er I may roam, however plac'd I may be,
My spirit instinctively turns unto thee."

Respectfully,   T. P, SLIDER.

PREFACE.

To a manuscript left by the Hon. A. P. Butler, which was sent to me by some person under the signature of "Stat Umbra Nominis," while I was engaged in penning biographical sketches of some departed men of worth, am I indebted for a record of the Butler family, and much of the traditionary information which is thrown forth in this little volume of incidents, anecdotes and stirring scenes that occurred in the dark hours of the Revolutionary struggle. In connection has been consulted many of the quaint old histories of those days, while traditional stories and incidents, gathered from aged patriarchs, have furnished me with material sufficient to have extended this little volume twice its size. I trust however, what has been written, though it bears the impress of hoary time, and is clad to some degree in the habiliments of tradition, may rise upon the mind of the reader, as he turns over its pages in some idle hour of "the progressive present" like "the swell of some sweet tune," awakening the imagination with melting strains "that now sink to mellow notes," now die away, and in mysterious unison touching some tender chord, without producing grief or regret, leaving its thrilling memory on heart and soul and ear.

THE AUTHOR.

INTRODUCTORY REMARKS.

Biography is the store-house of experience. Its chief value is in the helpful information it gives, making the reader better, wiser, happier and richer in historical events. Hence, it is the duty of a writer, who really desires to be of some assistance to his fellow-men ; when he undertakes to sketch the life of another, to write with truth and clearness. As such, our endeavor will be so, to entwine the history of the times and section in which the events occurred, with the biography of the patriotic partisan, that it cannot fail of being interesting and instructive to the young—pleasant and acceptable with the old. Suffice it, the person whom we are attempting to portray and place before you : threw his whole soul toward the accomplishment of national independence. He labored to break, if possible, the connection with the mother country, and open the way to the duties and advantages of popular government. National independence was the first epoch in our history; and such was its importance that Lafayette boasted to the first consul of France, that although its battles were but mere skirmishes in comparison with his, they decided the fate of the world. Casting a retrospective glance over the revolutionary history of our country, it is profoundly interesting to notice how the life-work of our revolutionary patriots appears to run naturally into the life-work of the nation ; until we almost seem to feel the warm, patriotic spirit of these noble men speaking to us telephonically, through decades of years in their heroic manliness,

" Strike till the last armed foe expires,
Strike for your altars and your fires."

In the management of God of the universe ; there are no accidents, from the fall of a sparrow to the fall of a nation ; from the movement of a planet to the sweep of a meteor. All is in accordance with the designs of Divine Providence, whose laws are mysterious and inscrutable. It was no accident which gave to South Carolina, in the trying times of her history, the patriots whom we now feel disposed to honor —Captain James Butler and his sons.

" Aye, honor decks the turf that wraps their clay."

It was no accident which took the father and his youngest son away so suddenly and violently from their patriotic duties and their home, and left one who was—

" To face fearful odds
For the ashes of his father
And the temple of his gods,"

fighting his way with vigilant eyes, ever watching his foes, who were prowling around him, and aiming their blows. If ever men sacrificed their health, fortunes and lives for their country's welfare, it was the members of this family. Two fell side by side, father and son ; and one, struggling amid the storms of fate, fought his way, like another Chevalier Bayard, to preserve those sacred rights which we now enjoy. If Kosciusko shone forth through the light of biographical narrative ; surely it will be no infringement on the rights of those who have remained unforgotten, that the subjects connected with this memoir, should not command a reverence equal to any, who figured in the arena for liberty. Scores of men spend their efforts and their lives in the public service, and yet are solely bent on serving themselves. The test of patriotism is in sacrificing self-interest to the interest of one's country. They,—only thought of the public good, simply, purely, constantly, devotedly and sacrificingly.

The accumulated force of centuries is with us. The gentle influences of Christianity, the broad and liberalizing tendency of modern culture, the immortal spirit of hopes and aspirations, crushed and buried beneath the ruins of past ages, with the profoundly interesting problem of self-government, is with us. The magnificent panorama, of thousands of cities, towns and villages, with their crowded population and stately structures of every character ; whose spires rise heavenward, and glisten and sparkle beneath the rays of the noonday sun ; with factories of every description, from which comes borne along on the wings of the breeze, as it flits on by, the shrill whistle of the engine and the clatter of machinery ; with radiating lines of railroads, from center to circumference, over which speeds the iron horse;

with the huge steamships and sailing vessels, carrying thousands of tons and cutting the waves of all oceans; with the telegraph, printing press, sewing machine, phonograph, papyrograph, electric light, and what not; with the illimitable acres of cultivated ground, enriched by golden heads of wheat, swelling ears of corn and snowy pods of cotton; with the millions—the bone and sinew of the country—engaged in manipulating the soil, wielding the hammer and the saw, the sound of which is heard on every side, is also with us; proving and demonstrating that we are moving forward to-day in the march of nations, proudly conscious of the importance of our mission; the sacred indestructibility of the country, and the principles for which just such men as we are describing, fought, bled and died. In the strictest sense, we are the heirs of all the ages,--and as we move forward in the gradual unfolding and development of our national life, we should remember, cherish and carry with us, in everything we do, a strong impetus, drawn from the struggles, the aspirations and hopes of the future, entertained by the gallant patriots of the past,

"Who waved the sword on high
And swore with her to live—with her to die."

GENERAL WILLIAM BUTLER,

The subject of this memoir, was born in Prince William county, Va., in 1759. His father, Captain James Butler, emigrated with his family to South Carolina, and settled in what was called then, the District of " 96," a few years before the opening of the Revolution. The circumstances of the times, pregnant then with the seeds of revolution, were such that every loyal-minded Whig was deeply interested in the affairs of the colonies. To doubt and waver was characteristic of the Tories. Captain Butler and his four sons were true patriots, imbued with the principle that—come what would—they would battle for the rights of the colonies to the death. The times grew warmer and warmer politically, and they prepared to take an active part in the scenes that were approaching. Actuated by a desire to put his house in order before the fury of the storm was upon him, he commenced to arrange his domestic affairs ; but before he had completed his arrangements, he was earnestly called upon to engage in the public concerns of the country. Without a moment's hesitation, he entered cheerfully in the snow-camp expedition under General Richardson. After this, he was with General Williamson in his expedition against the Cherokee Indians in 1779.

When the conflict which had been raging in the North was transferred by a new movement, as a change of base in warlike operations, of from North to South, the war may be said to have been inverted. Then it was the North was abandoned by the British for a time, and South Carolina and the adjacent settlements became the principal theatre of offensive operations. Upon the call for General Lincoln, who had been placed in command of the Southern forces, Captain Butler repaired at once to head-quarters, which was located near Augusta, Ga. Unfortunately he was taken sick, and became unable to follow the army in the subsequent campaign. From this period few events of revolutionary interest occurred in the upper districts of the State until after the fall of Charleston. The capitulation of the forces in the city, and the dispersion or retreat of the small detached corps which had kept the field during the siege, was regarded by the **royal commander** as a restoration of British authority, and both civil and **military organizations were arranged to maintain it.** The inhabitants of the State were called upon to swear allegiance to British authority and **take British protection.** The village of Ninety-six was designated as a place for the citizens of the surrounding country to appear at for this purpose The proclamation was considered delusive, and **many persons appeared on the specified day without fully understanding its import.** Among them was Captain James Butler, who, when informed of what was demanded of him, positively **refused to conform to the terms of the proclamation.** The British-officer in command immediately put him in irons and threw him in Ninety-Six jail, from whence he was transferred to Charleston, where- he was confined in the "provost" for 18 months. Upon his release from this severe and lengthened imprisonment, which occurred in the latter part of December, 1781, he returned once more to his home, where he remained about three weeks; when he was called on to seal with his life his devotion to the cause, for which he had already **suffered so much. The incidents of** the bloody **tragedy in** which he **died can be paralleled only in the annals of** civil **strife.**

From the beginning of the contest with the mother country, a difference of opinion had existed in the State upon the subject. **South Carolina had** been a province of the Crown. The grievances complained of by the commercial **colonies** were unfelt by her. The tories, or *scouilites*, insisted **that the** King had laid **no** new burdens or taxes on **the people, and that,** therefore, **their** opposition to the royal government was groundless. The act as it respected **South** Carolina was true, **but the conclusion** drawn from it did not follow. No new **burdens had been laid on the** inhabitants of the province of Carolina, but the **most grievous had been** laid on Massachusetts, in pursuance of principles which equally applied to Carolina, and struck at the foundation of her boasted rights. **The fact is,** a strong conservative feeling pervaded a large class of her people. This feeling was strongest in the **up-country. There the** inhabitants took arms from the beginning. Upon **both sides of the question there** were to be found rash, hard-headed, impulsive, **ignorant, prejudiced** men, and **the** contest became fierce, **merciless and bloody. Outrage** and tyranny, producing reprisals, as-

sumed a savage, guerrilla character, in which says General Greene:
"The inhabitants pursued each other like wild beasts, killing each
other, robbing each other without regard to age, condition or sex, as
well as plundering and firing barns, houses and whatever came to
hand."

A marauding party of royalists made an incursion into the neigh-
borhood of Mount Willing, in Edgefield District, near which Captain
Butler lived, carrying off considerable booty. The result was, a band of
Whigs was formed immediately for the pursuit and punishment of the
bandits. Captain Butler was called upon to take command of the
party. At first he positively refused to do so, alleging that the hardships and sufferings he had endured in prison had rendered him at
that time utterly unfit to take charge of such an expedition, and therefore should exempt him from the undertaking.

The majority of the men excused him on these grounds, but his son,
James Butler, one of the party, refused to continue with the expedition, unless his father assumed the command. Captain Butler yielded to the appeal of his son, and consented to go at his request, but
simply as an adviser ; the active command being in a man by the name
of Turner. Pursuit being instituted, the Royalists were overtaken, defeated and dispersed at Farrar's Spring, in Lexington District, S. C.,
and the horses and cattle, which they had captured, recaptured. On
their return with the captured booty, being highly exhilarated with
their success, and rendered more particularly so by an improper use
of peach brandy, which they had captured in the fight, they concluded
to stop at a place on Cloud's Creek for the night and encamp, not-
withstanding the appeals and urgent remonstrances of Captain Butler,
who insisted on moving forward all night. Finding his advice disre-
garded as to advancing, he counseled the necessity of the ordinary military precautions against surprise, of placing out sentinels, but they
turned a deaf ear to all advice. They were mostly young men, of but
little experience, yet confident, as youth is, and then the worst of it,
under the influence of liquor. Their success and indulgence had rendered them overweeningly reckless, conceited and careless, just as we
find them to-day. It was not known then exactly who were the loy-
alists, as they were sometimes called, they had pursued and whom
they had discomfited ; but the next morning demonstrated the wis-

dom and sagacity of the advice given by the gray-headed counselor, Captain Butler. They proved to have been a detached party connected with a larger band, for about sunrise this band,amounting to some three hundred men, guided by some of the escaped, discomfited party, under the lead, too, of one of the bravest and most skillful partisans of the Royal side, yet sanguinary, vindictive, relentless, and unforgiving, to-wit : Bloody Bill Cunningham was seen approaching, who at once attacked the camp. Taken almost by surprise, and by this to a certain degree disorganized, the little squad of imprudent Whigs, about thirty in number, nevertheless rallied for a moment and took refuge in an unfinished log house without doors or windows. In the meantime the house was surrounded by Cunningham's men when firing commenced. After a few moments of rapid discharges, a demand of surrender peremptorily was made. Its terms were inquired of by the Whigs, and the response was of the Tory leader, "they were unconditional", but that he would receive a communication from them. Upon this Smallwood Smith, one of the party, was, selected to perform the duty. Upon presenting himself, Cunningham's first inquiry was, Who are of your party ?

Upon learning that young James Butler, the son of Captain Butler, who had been engaged in an affair in which one Radcliff, a noted Tory was killed, was among them, he determined at once to give no terms that would exempt this young man from his vengeance. Cunningham was well acquainted with the father, having served with him in the expedition against the Indians, to which allusion has already been made. It is said that Cunningham had rather a strong liking and partiality for him, and would have entertained terms of friendly capitulation with the party had it not been for the presence of the son. Captain James Butler sent Cunningham a message that if he would spare the life of his son, he would make an unconditional surrender of himself, Young Butler, however, learning Cunningham's animosity to himself, and entertaining the impression that his father and himself would be sacrificed in the event of any surrender, determined to run all hazards of a contest of arms, and fearlessly informed his father that he would settle the terms of capitulation. So on the first opportunity that presented itself, he commenced the combat anew by killing a Tory by the name of Stewart. It is said that negotiations had been entered into to save the officers and sacrifice the privates ; but be this as it may, this demonstration of courage concluded the parley, and young Butler (but nineteen years of age,) received a mortal wound in the fierce conflict that followed, while kneeling to pick his flint for a discharge. The gallant, but expiring boy called his father, who had come upon the expedition at his request, unarmed, simply as a counselor, to his side, handed him his rifle and told him there were yet a few bullets in his pouch and to revenge his death. The father took the gun and discharged it against the enemy until the ammunition was expended. The death of young Butler produced a panic in the little party, contending against such hopeless odds, and the result was unconditional surrender. After a formal meeting and consultation of the officers of the Tory squad, under the guidance of the blood-thirsty and execrable chieftain Cunningham, the terrific order was issued to put them all to the unsparing sword of retaliation and revenge. Two of the number managed to escape ; the balance were shot down and slaughtered where they stood. Captain James Butler caught up a pitch-fork that was lying around and defended himself until his right hand was severed by a sabre stroke, and his life ended by a rifle ball. The tragedy did not cease here. A detachment of the Tories under the command of Prescott, a subordinate leader, was left to meet any burying party that might be sent to inter the bodies of the mangled victims and especially to meet the subject of our memoir, then a Captain of Rangers, who it was expected would hasten to the spot. But William Butler was too far from the sad locality to be present even at the funeral ceremonies.

In those days, when population was sparse and when the passions of men, like as to-day, embittered by fierce political strife, swelled to uncontrollable highths, smothering every kindly feeling, and engendering hate and animosity of the most malignant nature, it seemed utterly impossible for them to act upon the principles of mercy. love and charity. Under the circumstances and excitement of the times, it would have been madness and sheer folly for the Whigs, unless strongly supported, to have undertaken the burial of their dead without an agreement. In this crisis, when head strong passion got the reins of reason, like a ship dashed by fierce encountering tides becomes the sport of wind and wave. and there seemed no prospect or way of coming to any terms; for the Tories were relentless and determined, and the Whigs powerless to act, there appeared on the arena of strife a new actor; one who has played a prominent part in the history of the world; in the plucking of an apple in the Garden of Eden; the mothership of the Saviour, and the appropriation of gorgeous jewelry when kings refused to act; thereby aiding to develop and lay open to view by degrees along the shores of the unremitting stream of the centuries, that have glided into the present in the universe of God, for the benefit of man—a new continent and a new world that stands to-day at the head of nations. This actor was woman. Aye! it was woman who stepped between the combatants and advanced with more than Spartan courage and devotion to perform the rites of interment. It was woman with her wisdom who carried and decided the difficulty. Souls know no difference of sexes; though man may be said to be the lord, it does not follow he has the monopoly of brain or courage or patriotism. Many a masculine heart and more than masculine has been found in a female breast; nor is the treasure of wisdom, or any of the nobler characteristics, the less valuable for being lodged in the weaker vessel. Truthfully has the poet said

> " 'Tis woman's hand that smooths affliction's bed,
> Wipes the cold sweat and stays the sinking head."

Sages may teach, poets may sing, and philosophers reason, but nature made woman to temper man. Without her man would have been a brute—a savage—influenced by passions and appetites, living serpents that would have wound like the gorgons round him; strangling those virtues which constitute his happiness and cheers him on to a happier shore. In the darkest hour of man's earthly ills, her affection and her courage rises and glows

> "Throbs with each pulse, and beats with every thrill.

Mrs. Sarah Smith, a sister of Captain James Butler, the father, (whose wife at this time was confined to her bed) with a number of other ladies, wives, mothers and sisters of the dead, hastened to the bloody scene to engage in their burial; Captain Butler's body was recognized by his severed hand. The mangled and unmercifully beaten bodies of the rest were so disfigured that it was impossible to recognize them. However, young Butler was supposed to be identified by his female relatives present. To the honour of the women present be it said, that with spade and hoe in hand ; they set to work, dug the trench and consigned to their resting-place the bodies of the murdered Whigs, save Captain Butler and his son, who were placed in a separate grave, prepared by his sister and relatives, which was marked at the time, and over which, in after years, was reared an humble monument, the tribute of filal piety.

> "And though the mound that mark'd their names,
>   Beneath the wings of time,
> Has worn away ! Their's is the fame
>   Immortal and sublime,
> For who can tread on Freedom's plain
>   Nor wake her dead to life again."

It was about the time of this sad event that Gen. Lincoln issued a proclamation from his camp at Black's Swamp, near Augusta, that William Butler, the subject of this memoir, repaired to his standard as lieutenant of militia. The American leader's purpose was with the view, Ramsay says, of limiting the British to the sea coast of Georgia, as well as of its reclamation. Leaving a corps of observation at Purysburg, under Moultrie, he marched with the main army up the Savannah river, that he might impart confidence to the country, and crossed high up ; but he had scarcely done so, when his sagacious adversary Prevost, availing himself of the critical time, and finding his way open to Charleston, made a brilliant dash for the capture of that city, and had nearly succeeded. When Prevost crossed the Savannah river, Charleston was almost wholly defenceless. Such a move as an invasion on the land side was unexpected. Lincoln nevertheless Prevost's move, pursued his original intention, from an idea that Prevost meant nothing more than to divert him from his intended operations in Georgia, by a feint of attempting the capital of South Carolina. In the meantime Moultrie threw himself in his path, met him at Willisling and Coosawhatchee, and by a defensive, masterly retreat, delayed his advance until field works sufficient to withstand an assault could be thrown up for defence of the city. During these events Lincoln hastily marched back from the interior of Georgia, recrossed the Savannah river, and pushed on after Prevost with hasty strides, while Governor Rutledge, with 600 militia from Orangeburg, and Col. Harris, with 300 Continental troops from the vicinity of Augusta, were striving to get ahead of Prevost and reinforce Moultrie. Having a knowledge of these things, Prevost advanced to Watson's, about a mile from the lines. As the garrison were unprepared for a siege, they stood to their arms all night. Presuming that Lincoln was close behind Prevost, to gain time for his coming up, they sent a message to Prevost, requesting to know on what terms a capitulation would be granted ; this was a ruse. Whatever was the presumption of the Whigs, as to what effect this trick might have, on the next morning Prevost and his army were gone, retreating by way of the islands, to Savannah. The militia of the up-country were then discharged ; but William Butler, who was connected with the detachment engaged in the action at Stono, remained and attached himself to Pulaski's legion, in which he served the remainder of the campaign of 1779. He was with the gallant Pole until his death at the siege of Savannah, and always spoke of him as a bold, dashing dragoon officer, and complimented his memory by naming one of his grandson's after him.

During the captivity of his father in Charleston, already narrated, all the responsibilities of family obligations devolved on William Butler. It was at this time too, the time immediately succeeding the fall of Charleston, when sprang into existence that brilliant roll of partisan leaders—Marion, Sumter, Butler, Gandy, the Postells, Benson, Greene, Conyers, McCauley, McCottry, Ryan, Watson, and others of South Carolina, whose achievements threw such a halo of glory and gorgeous chivalry over the war in the South, that—

> " The tilt, the tournament, the vaulted hall,
> Fades in its glory on the spirit's eye,
> And fancy's bright and gay creation—all
> Sinks into dust, when reason's searching glance
> Unmasks the age of Knighthood and romance."

It was about this time that Washington appointed, at the request of Congress, General Greene to take command of the forces in the Southern District, which he did in August, 1780. From this time the depression and gloominess, which had settled like a funeral pall over the minds of many of the people upon the fall of Charleston, began to disappear, until it was entirely removed from public sentiment, and

South Carolina rose like a Phœnix from the ashes and became one of the most heroic and warlike colonies of the Revolutionary league.

General Greene's movements on Ninety-Six, is a matter of history. At that time William Butler was serving under General Pierson on the Carolina side of the Savannah river near Augusta. He was present at the siege of Augusta, and after the fall of that place, having been detailed by General Pickens to attend Colonel Lee to Ninety-Six, then being besieged also, he had the honor of being present at the interview between Greene and Lee, in which the latter suggested the attack upon the stockade. General Butler always expressed himself with much emphasis when speaking of this interview, repeating the words of Lee, "That the spring must be taken." To which Greene replied by saying, "How can it be done without a general assault?" Lee responded, "Allow me to take the stockade on the opposite side, and my guns will soon drive them from the water." The stockade was taken, and the garrison deprived of the use of the spring. An operation which it has been contended by military critics, if accomplished at a certain period of the siege, would have resulted in the fall of the place before it could have been relieved. As it was, Cruger, commanding the garrison, managed to prolong his defense by sinking wells in the star redoubt. Terms of capitulation had been proposed, which Green refused, believing he could still take the place by pushing the sap against the star redoubt. The approach of Lord Rawdon with a relieving force blasted his hopes. A corps was detached to meet Rawdon, while an assault upon an incomplete breach was hazarded. Some skirmishing between Rawdon's advance guard and this corps took place near Saluda Old Town, in which some were killed and several wounded. A young lieutenant from Virginia, by the name of Wade, was shot, and as he fell from his saddle, for he was mounted—with a genuine trooper's care for his steed—forgetting himself—he exclaimed to his comrades, "Don't let my horse, boys, fall into the hands of the enemy." Fortunately there was a settler close by, by the name of Sam Savage, to whose house he was removed.

The American forces fell back, and marched toward the Enoree river. But a short time after this little skirmish, a young dragoon officer who was in pursuit of Greene, with a white plume and the cockade of the Whigs in his hat, accompanied by an orderly, rode up to Savage's, where the wounded young lieutenant was lying, made inquiries, and learned from his step daughter in the house, who had just returned from the vicinity of Ninety-Six, that the siege was raised, and that Greene's forces had fallen back in full retreat, crossed Saluda at the Island Ford, with Lee's legion bringing up the rear. This young officer was Captain William Butler, and, strange to say, this was his first meeting with the lady, whom he subsequently married. He had been detached from the army at Ninety-Six some weeks before, upon some separate service under General Henderson, from whom he derived his commission as captain in 1781. He determined in his mind at once to join the retreating army, and being told that two stragglers from Rawdon's command were down in Savage's low grounds taking the plantation horses, he took them prisoners, and, mounting one of them behind himself and the other behind his orderly, swam the Saluda river near what is now called Bozeman's Ferry, and joined Lee about ten miles from the Island Ford on the Newberry side. He learned from the prisoners that Rawdon had pushed forward a strong light corps, embracing cavalry and infantry, in hot pursuit of the retreating Americans.

When William Butler came up with Lee, he informed him of the pursuit, and the information came none too soon. Lee had halted his command, and was lying on his saddle blanket, making a pillow of the saddle. His prompt direction to Armstrong, one of his captains, as soon as he received the information, was, " Form your troop in the rear and fight while we run." The legion was barely on the march when the enemy appeared, but Armstrong made the required demonstration with such gallantry and confidence that the enemy, apprehending an engagement with a stronger force, paused for reinforcements, and Lee was enabled to put himself in closer communication with the main body, which was then halted at Bush Creek. After this time, William Butler became a partisan, sometimes serving as second in command under Ryan, and sometimes in the same position under Watson, both partisan leaders of local distinction. At a subsequent period he raised and commanded a company of mounted rangers, under a commission from General Pierson, confirmed by the Governor of the State. While serving under Watson, he was engaged in an expedition against a band of Tories, who had organized themselves on the Edisto. The expedition rendezvoused at the ridge in Edgefield,

District. Michael Watson, the leader, was a determined, resolute, yet revengeful man, and controlled too much by the influences which these feelings suggested. When they met the Tories at Drow Swamp, the latter were stronger than had been expected, and occupied a well fortified position. Nettled and somewhat exasperated at finding he had been entrapped, instead of being governed by discretion, he pushed on, disdaining a retreat. The consequence was, his men fell back at the first fire, with symptoms of panic, and made a faltering response to his order to charge. But few obeyed with the ready alacrity with which they were want to welome it. Many obeyed not at all. The result was a second order, and they were driven back again; then the stern old warrior, maddened, and shouting in stentorian tones his "rally," ordered his men to charge, or woe to the man who failed to do his duty; but only about fifteen men came up to the call. They had gone into the fight against superior numbers, strongly posted in the swamp; which position they still maintained. Watson now became furious, and losing his judgment, persisted in his attempts. At length, while loading his rifle behind a tree, he was mortally wounded by a ball through his hip. William Butler, at this decisive moment, assumed the command, giving his lieutenancy to a man by the name of John Corley. The extreme danger in which the party had been placed by the rashness of Watson required a resort to desperate measures, so he placed Corley in the rear, with an order to cut down the first man who gave way. It so happened that Joseph Corley, a brother of the one first spoken of, with others was seen to fall back, which, if it had been overlooked, would have doomed the fate of the balance to certain destruction. John Corley, true to the orders of his leader, drew his pistol, and placing the muzzle at the head of his brother, ordered him back to his post. Joseph returned without a dissenting word, and conducted himself afterward gallantly throughout the fight. During the affray, a man by the name of Vardell was mortally wounded, and before the breath left him, begged his comrades not to let his body fall into the hands of the Tories. Watson, lying between the contending parties, made a similar request, especially to William Butler. "Billy, my brave boy," exclaimed the wounded partisan chief, "Do not let the cussed Tories take my body."

Desperate and reckless, Butler and his men, with a wild, demoniac shout that rang out on the welkin as from so many furies, made a terrible charge that bore down everything before it, scattering the tories on the right and left, and succeeded also in bringing off their dead and wounded comrades. As they retreated, they found time to bury the body of Vardell, concealing it under the roots of a large oak which had fallen, covering it over with dirt and leaves by the use of their swords. At some little distance from the scene of the conflict, they took refuge in a log house, which answered the purpose of a block-house and resting place. Watson, though sorely wounded, and under the apprehension of death, still maintained a determined resolution. A woman happened to be found in the house in which they had taken shelter, whose infant, five weeks old, was in a dwelling house some little distance off. Watson insisted that she should be detained, as their peculiar condition and weakness required concealment if possible, as he said, she might betray them ; but she, finding this out, hooted at the idea of betraying her Whig friends. Through her they found means, however, to convey information of their whereabouts, and their perilous situation, to Orangeburg, where there was a detachment. Captain (subsequently) General Rumph, as soon as apprised, hastened to their relief. Under his escort Watson was carried upon a litter, in a dying condition, to Orangeburg Court House, where he expired, and was buried with military honors, Captain Butler superintending.

After this, we find the subject of this memoir acting as lieutenant with Ryan. Here he engaged in another expedition against the Tories in Orangeburg District. The Whigs were in force near the court house. A number of Tories, believing their condition perilous, and their cause on the wane, deserted to the Whig force. Ryan, distrusting them, gave orders in an engagement to place them in front, with positive instructions if they wavered for his men to shoot them down. In a fight that occurred they proved true, but Ryan was disabled by a shot, and Lieutenant Butler assumed the command. The Tories here were signally defeated.

In 1782, Cunningham, the celebrated Tory partisan, made a second incursion into the 96th District. Perfectly familiar with the country from his youth, possessed of great sagacity and fertility of genius in military expedients, wary and strategetic, endowed with all the physi-

cal qualities so essential to a partisan, withal bold, dashing and reckless, he was even, if a Tory, a dangerous as well as a formidable adversary to contend with. A favorite manœuvre of his was to divide
his command upon the march into small detachments, to be concentrated after the Napoleonic plan by different routes, meeting, as near
as could be calculated upon, close to or at the point at which his blow
was aimed. In this manner he had concentrated his forces at Corrodine's
Ford on the Saluda. William Butler, who was then commanding a
company of rangers under the authority of General Pickens, with a
portion of his men, manœuvered to come upon him, if possible, and
take him by surprise. With a view to ascertain Cunningham's position, he resorted to a ruse. Approaching the residence of Joseph Cunningham near the junction of the little Saluda and big Saluda, he
sent forward his brother, Thomas Butler, with Abner Corley, to the
house in the night. Thomas Butler was an excellent mimic, so when
he came in hailing distance of the house, he called aloud, imitating
the voice of one of William Cunningham's men, named Niblett, and
asked where our friend Cunningham was? The wife of Joseph Cunningham, coming to the door, replied, "That he had crossed Corrodine's
Ford." With this information, William Butler himself rode up to the
house, and finding Joseph Cunningham there, compelled him, on peril
of his life, to guide the party across the ford. They crossed the ford
at 12 m. that night, and next morning halted in a peach orchard, near
Bouknight's Ferry, on the Saluda. The horses were unbitted with
saddles on, and were feeding upon peas out of a caddy, when a gray
mare, which Cunningham was known to have taken from the neigh-
borhood, was observed passing back, having escaped from the camp.
This incident disclosed, in some measure, the state of affairs, and the
Rangers received the orders to march. The Rangers numbered some
thirty, and Cunningham's men some twenty. The bloody transaction
of Cloud's Creek.

"Feeding its torch with the thought of wrong,"

aroused the passion, stirred up the blood and enthused the chivalrous
spirit of Butler, to grapple with the bloody fiend and wreak if possible
vengeance for the deed. It was not the vengeance as sought for by
an assassin. It was not to be taken in a dastardly manner ; no mid-

night shot gun from behind a tree, or the sudden plunge of a sharp
knife; the coward's virtue, through the heart--no ! It was an encounter to be like as between the knights of old; an encounter rather with
the feelings of the duello than the battle field. Approaching the partisan's position, John Corley was detailed with eighteen men to gain
the rear, and upon a concerted signal to commence the attack. While
the main body advanced under cover of a hedge, the Tories were dry-
ing their blankets by their camp fires, and Cunningham himself was
at a little distance off from his band. As it afterwards appeared,
Butler's person being at one time exposed, in advancing before the signal was given, he was observed by the Tories, but taken for their own
leader, for it is said there was a strong personal resemblance between the two men. Upon the giving of the signal, Corley made a
furious and dashing assault, himself foremost, like another Murat in
leading the charge

> "Thus joined the band, whom mutual wrong,
> And fate and fury drove along."

This was the first intimation to the Tories that their exasperated
foes were at hand. Cunningham was promptly at his post ; but although taken by surprise, his eyes were open, and he saw at a glance
that his foes were superior in numbers ; but so wary was he,

> "By trial of his former harms and cares,"

governed too by the adage that "discretion is the better part of valor,"
that he shouted out to his men to take care of themselves, and hastened to his saddleless steed, released the bridle reins, and then on
her bare back nimbly leaped astraddle, with a trained partisan's quick-
ness, and went bounding through the wild woods like another Mazep-
pa. Close behind him dashed Butler in hot pursuit. Nothing could
have been more exciting, and more to have been desired by him

> "Away !--away ! and on they dash !
> Torrents less rapid and less rash."

Both men were remarkably fine riders, and tradition has preserved
the names of the two horses they rode on that occasion. Cunningham
was mounted on a stylish, splendidly formed black mare having glossy
skin, trim legs, with three white feet.

> "Who looked as though the speed of thought
> Were in her limbs,"

that had become celebrated in his service as "Silver Heels," while Butler rode a noble-looking, broad-breasted, long-hoofed, straight legged,
passing strong steed, a dark bay, with full eyes and nostrils wide,
called "Ranter," who possessed great powers of endurance. Butler
carried only a sabre, and Cunningham pistols which had been rendered useless by the rain of the previous night, for he snapped them
both repeatedly over his shoulders at his adversary as the gallant mare
went thundering on

> "With flowing tail and flying mane
> With nostrils never stretched by pain."

Life or death to both hung upon the fleetness of their horses. As
long as the chase was in the woods, Ranter maintained his own ; but
when they struck an open trail, in which the superior stride of Cunningham's thorough-bred, could tell, turning his body, with his head
thrown round, looking over his left shoulder askance at Butler, hold-
ing tightly the reins in his left hand, while a trumphant smile played
over his countenance, he patted the shoulders of the noble animal that
bore him, tauntingly exclaiming, as he threw out his right hand behind him, shaking his forefinger—"Damn you, Bill Butler, I'm safe ;
but mark, the next chase will be mine !,' when

> Away ! away ! dashed Silver heels
> Upon the pinions of the wind,
> Leaving Ranter far behind;
> She sped like a meteor thro' the sky
> When with its crackling sound the night,
> Is chequer'd with the northern light,

and soon was seen with her rider on her back swimming Saluda river
near Lorick's Ferry. Sullenly Butler returned from the pursuit of
Cunningham. At the Tory camp he found a portion of his command
assembled under circumstances which gave him great concern. Turner, one of the Tory prisoners, had been deliberately shot through the
heart after he had surrendered. Alas !

> "There's was the strife
> That neither spares nor speaks for life."

Upon inquiry he ascertained one Seysin had done the deed, who
justified himself by reciting an outrage the unfortunate man had in-
flicted upon his mother, to-wit : Turner had stripped Mrs. Seysin to

the waist, then tied her hard and fast, and whipped her severely to force her to disclose where was concealed a party of Whigs, among whom was her son. Butler sternly rebuked the act as cruel and contrary to the rules of civilized warfare. Though warring against a savage, relentless foe, yet he was high-toned and chivalrous to a fault. Seysin was brought to trial before the corps. The verdict was in his favor and no court martial was held. The deed was certainly savage and cruel, but the strong, palliating circumstances of the whipping of his mother was in his favor.

A pursuit of Cunningham's men was ordered immediately by Butler for the purpose of capturing or finally dispersing them. Some were overtaken while crossing the river and some in the forest. Butler was disposed to be lenient and merciful, but he soon saw that his men, rough, illiterate and prejudiced, were ungovernable. Such is, and has ever been, the result of civil strife. Alas! the horrors of war when a common country is divided.

> "All that the Devil would do, if run stark mad,
> Is then let loose.

No threats or orders could deter them from shooting the fleeing Tories. He ordered one DeLoach, who was in the act of firing his rifle, to desist; while another by the name of Sherwood Corley, who was just behind him in the river, snapped his pistol at one of the retreating Tories, and though he was ordered to cease from firing, yet deliberately reprimed his rifle afresh, fired and killed a Tory by the name of Davis as he was ascending the Edgefield bank.

> "In vain he did whatever a chief may do
> To check the headstrong fury of that crew.
> In vain their stubborn ardor he would tame.
> But, alas!
> The hand that kindled could not quench the flame."

The result of this action was the breaking up and final dispersion of Cunningham's famous band. He himself retired to Cuba, where he was awarded after his arrival something like an ovation by the British for his traitorous services. After the war, Major Gandy, a gallant partisan of the Revolution, visited Cuba on account of his health. Cunningham in the true spirit of hospitality called upon him, and while chatting with him about the war, told him that on one occasion he had ridden up with an escort at his back to a house near Ninety-Six, in which Gandy and others were playing cards, with a view of ascertaining if William Butler was among them.

"Why did you not fire upon us?" asked Gandy.

"I had no desire to kill you," replied Cunningham, "but if Bill Butler had have been there, the floor of that house would have been flooded with blood.

Cunningham, before he left, extended an invitation to the Major to dine with him. Whether he did so or not tradition does not say. Here he died. He was a man born to command, of an unyielding and independent obstinacy of character, possessed of splendid military ability, bold, courageous, yet revengeful and vindictive. He might have won for himself an imperishable name of honor, but by his treason he wiped it out in the betrayal of his country, and his name remains to the ensuing age abhorred.

From the conclusion of this skirmish and the blotting out of Cunningham's band, until the close of the war, Butler continued at the head of the Rangers under the command of General Pickens, and was considered his favorite captain. He had, however, now very little duty to do, other than patrol to perform, consequently—

> "The trenchant blade, Toledo trusty,
> Grew rusty."

His company of Rangers was not discharged until after 1784, a year after the peace.

With the resumption of peace and the pursuits of civil life, the soldier's thoughts turned from—

> "The burning shell, the gateway wrench'd asunder,
> The rattling musketry, the clashing blade,
> The charge, the shout, the tones of thunder,
> The diapason of the cannonade,"

and reverted to the young girl of the Saluda—the star of his worship—

> "Whose gentle ray
> Beam'd constant o'er his lonely way,"

whom he saw at Savage's house during Greene's retreat from Ninety-Six, which has already been narrated; nor had she forgotten the young officer of the cockade and plume, for when the mother and

family bitterly opposed his attentions, and her step-father forbade
him to visit her at his house, she boldly and fearlessly proved by her
determination and pluck that—

> ' Love is not reasoned down or lost ;
> It grows into the soul,
> Warms every vein and beats in every pulse,''

for she told him to come and she would meet him. The result of it
was they were married in the latter part of 1784. Miss Bethethland
Foote Moore, whom William Butler had selected as his partner, as
the wife of his bosom, was a woman of strong, and in many respects
remarkable, traits of character. She always exercised great influence
over him, and he relied upon her judgment and advice. He seemed
to have inspired her with a deep and profound feeling of respect, almost amounting to fascination, which of itself is one of the highest
tributes that could be paid his memory.

In 1794, William Butler was elected by the Legislature of South
Carolina, which was then the custom, to be the sheriff of 96th District. He discharged few of the ministerial duties, however, leaving
these to be carried out by his brothers, Thomas and Stanmore, who
were his deputies ; but, as to one thing, he always conducted the military escort of the judge during the sitting of the courts. The sher-
iffalty of that day was an office of high distinction. It was esteemed
as an office of honor, which could only be obtained by men of virtue,
merit, honesty and worth, but now it hath lost its lustre and reputation, and resolved itself into a mercenary purchase.

William Butler, as sheriff of 96th District, received General Washington when upon his Southern tour, from the authorities of Georgia,
and conducted him by the Pine House to the Ridge in Edgefield District which was near the termination of his territorial jurisdiction. At
the Ridge, General Hampton, then sheriff of what was called Camden
District, received and conducted him to Granby, situated on the Con-
garee river, about one mile and a half below Columbia, through by
Camden, and thence to Charlotte, North Carolina, where the authorities of that State received the illustrious patriot and Father of his
Country.

In 1798 General Pickens resigned the office of Major-General of the
Upper Division of South Carolina militia, and through his recom-

mendation William Butler was elected by the State Legislature to fill
the vacancy. In 1800, General Butler became a candidate for Congress against Goodloe Harper, the incumbent from the 96th District.
Mr. Harper had been a Republican, but from conscientious motives joined the Federals, and supported what was peculiarly unpop-
ular at the South, " Jay's treaty." This raised opposition to him at
home, and General Butler was elected as the opposition candidate, his
old commander, John Ryan, moving the nomination. He succeeded
in the election, and took his seat in 1801. When the resolution charg-
ing General Wilkinson with complicity with Burr in his attempted
treason was moved and adopted in the House of Representatives,
the occasion gave rise to great sensation. A discussion took place
upon the floor of the House as to the Chairman of the Committee
of Investigation. A ballot was called for by Wilkinson's friends.
The motion was overruled, and the duty of making the appointment
devolved on the Speaker. He appointed General Butler. Wilkinson
at the time made some offensive remarks, something of this kind
" That he was not only to be tried by a militia General, but that he
was condemned before he was tried." This being reported to General
Butler, he resigned his position on the committee. Roger Bacon was
appointed to succeed him. Owing to the remarks, unfriendly communication passed between him and Wilkinson. They, however, in
course of time became reconciled.

In 1813. General Butler resigned his seat in Congress, distinctly and
conclusively, in preference of all others, to Mr. John C. Calhoun, the
great Southern statesman, saying to him, " You can meet Randolph in
debate—I cannot." How few would acknowledge so candidly their in-
feriority to-day, and resign their seat in Congress to put in even a Clay,
Webster or another Calhoun. That was the age of giants and
men. Verily, the days of nobleness of soul and pure integrity have
passed away. Each one at the present thinks he is the observed of the
observers. Cicero, Demosthenes, Patrick Henry, aye, Solomon, the
wise man, was a fool beside them.

Butler's admiration for Randolph was very high, and notwithstand-
ing they differed in opinion as to the war of 1812, they continued to
entertain friendly relations. Butler on a certain occasion spent sometime with him at his homestead, by invitation, in returning from Con-

gress. In 1814, General Butler was called by Governor Alston, in a very complimentary manner, now on record in Washington, to command the troops of South Carolina at Charleston. President Madison had in 1812 offered to him the commission of Brigadier-General in the United States army, but he declined it, saying, " He was a Major-General at home." General Jackson was appointed to command the forces at New Orleans, while General Butler was in command at Charleston. They had been comrades in early life, and Jackson sent him word, " That they were both called militia generals, but that he knew whichever was attacked first would do his duty. General Pickens, who was a man of some military ability, had an idea that he knew exactly how, as unfortunately was the case during the late civil strife, by a goodly lot of persons, to prescribe the mode of defense for Charleston, which was this : To allow the enemy to land and then fight them through the streets from behind barricades. Butler's response to him was, " That when he assumed the command, he expected to consult the dictates of his own judgment, and he should meet them at the water." An incursion was made upon one of the islands for the purpose of supplying provisions to the fleet off the coast, and a slight affair occurred, in which Captain Dent, of the navy, was principally engaged. The incursion was repelled. This was the only engagement with the enemy of any portion of General Butler's command. It had fallen to the lot of his friend to vindicate the ability of militia generals. The war terminated with the battle of New Orleans, and General Butler became a private citizen. From this period to the close of his life, he confined himself principally to the business of superintending his farm. During the time he was in Congress, his seat was twice contested. First, by Dr. Seriren, a man of high character, and afterward by Edmond Bacon, a man of decided ability. The last contest gave rise to the unfortunate issue known as "old and new parties of Edgefield." It was bitter and acrimonious, and led to many painful contentions. Mr. Bacon, however, became not only reconciled with, but afterwards a warm friend of General Butler and others, whose names are to be found upon the journal to consider the adoption of the Federal Constitution, and they voted against it. He was subsequently a member of the convention which formed the State Constitution, that held its own until changed by the Republican party of 1868.

General Butler's brothers were first, Thomas, who was regarded a man of considerable military talent ; second, Sampson, who was sheriff of Edgefield, and for many years a representative from that district in the State Legislature ; Stanmore, who was a captain in the United States army during the time war was expected with France, and was also clerk of the Court of Edgefield when he died ; and last, was James, who was killed during the Revolution in the skirmish on Cloud's creek. He had two sisters, Nancy and Elizabeth. The first married Elisha Brooks, who was a lieutenant in the Revolution ; the latter married Z. Smith Brooks, who was also a lieutenant in the Revolution., and subsequently a colonel of State cavalry. He had eight children, to-wit : James, who was sheriff of Edgefield District and a colonel of State cavalry at his death. George Butler was a lawyer, and during the war of 1812 served as major in the regular army. William was a physician, and was a surgeon in the army at New Orleans ; he also served one term as a representative in Congress. Frank Butler was a lawyer. Pierce M. Butler was an officer in the regular army; was president of the Bank of the State of South Carolina—was Governor of South Carolina, and fell in the battle of Churubusco, in Mexico, at the head of the gallant Palmetto regiment ; Emmela, the only daughter, was married to General Waddy Thompson, who was a lawyer, a member of Congress, and Minister to Mexico. Leontine died young. Andrew Pickens Butler, who passed away a score of years ago, and whom I knew well, was admitted to the practice of the law at an early age, rose to distinction in his profession, was elected a Judge by the South Carolina Legislature, and was finally elected by the same body as Senator to Congress, where he attained an enviable position.

General Butler was a handsome man. He stood fully six feet high. He was a good shot with the rifle, well versed in woodcraft and a splendid horseman. His love for horses amounted to a passion. He would have nothing but the finest blood on his place. He considered it a defect in his sons not to ride well, and was in the habit of making them break his colts, until upon one occasion, when a dare-devil filly was to be broken and two of the boys, Pickens and Pierce, were drawing lots to see who should have the honor of doing it, Mrs. Butler interfered saying, she could stand it no longer ; that they were her children as well as his, and if the filly was to be broken, why not let the negro boys do it. General Butler yielded, carelessly remarking in a humorous tone, with a smile playing around his mouth, "Well, my dear wife, be it so, but it would not hurt the boys to be thrown off, as the ground has just been freshly plowed." "No, mother," exclaimed the boys at the same time. "a little exercise to-day would be beneficial." At one time he was engaged upon the turf, and was in most cases suc- cessful. Upon one occasion, when he had entered into an engage- ment to run a race, some circumstance happened, by his financially assisting a friend, that run him short. Under the circumstances, how- ever, as his word was his bond, he put up as a *bona fide* collateral a favorite family body servant, whose name was Will. It annoyed him in no small degree, that he had to put him up. But as the vulgar adage runs, "Fortune favors the brave," so it seemed with him. He won the race. It was his last. Returning home satisfied and rejoiced, he communicated to his wife what had taken place. Upon hearing his statement, she read him a curtain lecture on the evils likely to result from horse-racing and gambling, and then solicited a pledge from him to the effect that he would never run another horse race or gamble. Forthwith he gave his pledge never to be guilty of the like again.

Having retired from all public business, and in a great degree hav- ing abandoned the most of his old habits, as horse-racing and sporting in general, he became almost a stranger in the midst of society, amusing himself with agricultural experiments, and in trying to pro- mote the happiness of his children and domestics, friends and neigh- bors. His health, which for sometime had been delicate, owing to the exposure and hardships endured during the war, gradually declined, and he passed away on the 23rd of September, 1821, in the beginning of his 63d year, with remarkable calmness, composure and dignity,

"Like one who draws the drapery of his couch
About him, and lies down to pleasant dreams."

While he left but little of anything that can be gathered from his- torical statements that is and was remarkable and more wonderful than can be said of thousands of others, yet what may be and has been penned by his son, as well as confirmed by many old citizens, who well recollected of him in the years gone by when I made inquiries, was that he was a man of note and decided mark in his day and time.

General Butler was a man of but little education, yet of strong impressions and great self-reliance. One strong peculiarity marked his public, as well as private character, which it would be well for many of the members of the Legislature, as well as of Congress, of much less calibre to model after. He had an utter contempt for long letters and long speeches. He frequently, when conversing on this subject, alluded to John Rutledge as one among the best speakers he ever heard, commending him chiefly for his brevity. He himself, whenever he addressed his constituents or an assembly, always made brief, pointed speeches, and he never wrote a letter over a page long, and that to the point. His sheriff books were a model of official exactness. During his life neither gain nor personal aggrandizement had any power to bend his principles and independence. In his political conflicts, no breath of suspicion ever assailed his integrity or dimmed the escutcheon of his honor. He could not have been induced to vary on any cherished opinion, except confronted by sound reasons, for the highest positions. Fawning and flattery were foreign to his nature. Keenly alive to any breath upon the purity of his motives, ancestry or character, he took no pains to cultivate notoriety. He was no literary scholar nor fluent orator. Though his connection with most of the events narrated was a subordinate one, yet he always had his own decided, determined opinions. Possessed of an excellent judgment, trained and educated in the academy of common sense, and graduating in the college of experience, which to mortals is a blessing and providence, he might truly be put down as a scholar of rare and undoubted might. As to his courage, he was as brave as humanity could possibly be. He had his faults; it would be fortunate for any of us who could be charged with less, but the error and frailty which belonged to him often took their color from virtue itself. On these he needs no silence, even if the grave, which has long been closed over him, did not refuse its echoes, except to what is good.

His reputation was the product of no hot-bed appliances, as used at the present day, but slowly and noiselessly it grew, strong and high, like the tall pine of his native country and State, whose head revels proudly in the sweeping winds. As an office-holder, he was courteous, respectful, and attended to the wants and requirements of his constituents. As a citizen, he was law-abiding, loyal and true. As a son, obedient and submissive. As a brother, his love was like that of Jonathan for David. As a husband, he was affectionate, devoted and constant. As a father, kind, loving and considerate, though he was absolute master of his household, making his children entirely subservient to his commands. As a friend, though his friendship was not demonstrative, yet it was strong and enduring. As a foe, he was manly and honorable. As a man, would there were more like him.

Silently in the deep stillness of that dreamless state which knows no waking earthly joys again, he reposes in the old burying ground on Big creek, in Edgefield District, S. C., while from the silence of the tomb and from the dust and bones that may lie in the coffin that contains them, there come forth lessons of warning and admonition, speaking in tones of thunder, fraught with experience and wisdom to the youth of his native State, who are just entering private and public life, with all its temptations and seducements before them; that there are tricks and shams and intimidations that are and will be set as pitfalls in their paths. With much that may be noble and inspiring about them, there are and will be manifold inclinations to sloth, to fickleness, and it may be to corruption. Who can tell whether some of them have not already set their feet in the way that leads down to moral death. They need the tones of that voice, whom we are now reviewing. which never directed the coward's retreat, the splendid calm of that clear face and blue eye, that kept its serenity and brilliancy amid all dangers and difficulties in the times that tried men's souls, and when the battle by day or night around him was at its thickest. They need the actual sight of and association with all such as he was, who by example and precept will elevate their aims, establish their character and make them truly patriotically private as well as public servants for the public good. And for those who are connected with public affairs to-day, and who desire to maintain and preserve an honorable reputation, what better course can be suggested or given than for those to emulate the patriotism, the steadfastness, the courage, the manliness, the sobriety, the honesty and the justice of William Butler !

> He speaks in characters that never die,
> The human greatness of an age gone by.

Butler
1556
1612

Walter   LeBoteler   Butler
1199

DeClare

Buteiller   1056
Latinized

Pinzerna
(Cup bearer)

le Boteler, Butler

See Virginia Historical Genealogies
By John B. Boddie - P. P. 17-32

Page 18 - Robert le Boteler, or
Robertus Pincerna grandson
of Richard Fitz-Gilbert
de Clare, Count d'Eu,
better known as Bien Fait
le Clare, came to England
where he became known as
Pincerna, or Robert le Boutiller,
he had two sons the elder
was Hervius Walter le
Boutilleur who became Baron
of Dunmow and Lord of
Bayard's Castle in London,
Hervius was the ancestor
of the Ormond Branch. His
son Hervius Walter le
Boutilleur became Walter
le Butler and went to
Ireland with Henry II or

England where he received large grants of land in the Province of Ormond and was named Chief Butler of Ireland. Later his line became the Earls and Dukes of Ormond. The younger son, brother of Hervius Walter was — Robert le Boutiller, or as he spelled it le Bûteler settled in Worcestershire and became the ancestor of George Boteler or Butler of Bedfordshire, John Boteler or Butler of Essex, the Kent Ireland Maryland Butlers, Jane Butler first wife of Augustine Washington and General William Butler of South Carolina.

On Page 26 Virginia

Historical Genealogies –

II. John Butler, d. 1684 is
the father of Major Caleb
Butler whose daughter
Jane Butler was the first
wife Augustine Washington
and mother of Augustine II
and Lawrence.

See Memoirs of General
William Butler Page 26 –
"In 1794 William Butler
was elected by the Legislature
of South Carolina which
was then the custom, to be
Sheriff of the 96th District"
Should be – In 1791
William Butler was
elected by the Legislature
of South Carolina which
was then the custom, to
be sheriff of th 96th District.
– In 1794 elected General of

he state militia.

See Historical Southern
Families - By John B. Boddie
Volume I - P.p. 13, 16

Corrections -

P. 13 Captain James Butler,
born 1723 - should be Capt.
James Butler, born 1738.

V. Elizabeth Butler, b. Dec. 17, 1776,
m. Zachariah Smith Moore —
should be - Zachariah Smith
Brooks

Page 14 - VII. Emmala Butler,
b. Aug. 24, 1800, m. Edmund
Bacon — should be - m.
Waddy Thompson

Other reference material -
See - South Carolina Historical
and Genealogical Magazine.
Vol. IV No. 4 - October 1903

Chronicles of Oklahoma
Spring 1952 - Pierce Mason

Butler

- Advancing the Frontier -
By Grant Foreman
- Pioneer Days in the Early
Southwest - By Grant Foreman
- Sequoyah - By Grant Foreman
- Southeastern Indians by
Emma Lila Funderburk
- George Washington - By
Foreman Volume 1, P.P. 33
and 34 - Jane Butler

Virginia Historical Genealogies
By Boddie
P. 18 le Boteler Arms :-
argent, on a chief indented
sable three covered cups
or.

Pincerna Arms :- Gules
three covered cups or -
Butiller latinized Pincerna
or Cupbearer - The name

Pincerna appears thrice in
Domesday Book - Pincerna
cupbearer to the King sealed
with a covered cup, his
successors assumed the
name le Botiler, le Boteler
and finally Butler - It
by no means follows that
all Butlers are descended
from Pincerna as all noblemen
as well as William the first
kept his butler -

V. H. G. Page 18 Nicholas
Butteler of Yatton married
his kinswoman Jane Butler
daughter and heir of John
Butler of Droitwich -
John Butler's arms :- Gules,
a chevron sable between
three covered cups or -
Crest :- A falcon rising or.
George Boteler or Butler
married Mary Throckmorton

d Jane Butler, first
d of Augustine
ashington –

Pierce Butler
Nashville, Tenn.
July 1966

11

Thomas Pinceena
supporters

Lower right ÷
Letter Seal of
Colonel Pierce
M. Butler,
South Carolina

Butler
1385 About

le Boteler
1149

Le Boteler
1199

Sigillum Thomas Pinceerna

Lower right ÷
Letter Seal of
Colonel Pierce
M. Butler,
South Carolina

Butler
1556
1612

Walter   le Boteler   Butler
1199

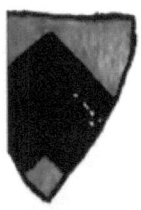

e Clare

Buteiller   1055
Latinized

Pinxerna
(Cup bearer)